Never Give Up

Cally Finsbury & Timothy Finsbury

DEDICATION

To all my wonderful helpers.

CONTENTS

1   Never Give Up   1

ACKNOWLEDGMENTS

To all my wonderful helpers.

Timothy had a sad look on his face and he was feeling rather glum.

His mother wanted to know what was wrong, but she waited, for she hoped Timothy would come to her when he was ready.

Timothy didn't stick to his usual routine. He wandered aimlessly around the house.

He ignored the cat.

He walked past the television.

He didn't pick up his device.

He walked into the garden and glanced around.

A sudden movement caught Timothy's eye.

He looked more closely and noticed it was a spider. His eyes continued to gaze at the spider as it began to weave its web.

The spider seemed extremely confident as it spun each part of the web.

"Timothy?" called Timothy's mum.

Timothy replied, "Coming!"

Timothy went inside and smiled when he was greeted with a warm and welcoming smile and a tasty snack waiting for him.

Later, when Timothy went into the bathroom he saw something, "Mum! Mum!" Timothy yelled.

Timothy's mum came at once and looked at what Timothy was pointing to.

There, in the bath, was a rather large spider.

With Timothy's shouting, the spider was startled frozen and did not move.

Timothy and his mum took a step back and just watched the spider.

Eventually, the spider began to move. It moved its many legs and it moved to many parts of the bath. The spider tried to climb up the side of the bath and made it up ever so slightly but then it slipped.

The spider tried again and again but each time it slipped back down to the base of the bath.

Timothy and his mum continued to observe the spider.

"There were so many instructions and I tried to make the picture but I just couldn't do it. All the other children seemed to get it and understand the instructions so easily. I just felt awful and started to cry."

Looking at the struggling spider reminded Timothy about his day at school, "Mum, today was really hard for me. We had to log on to the computers and get to a specific page."

Just at that moment, Timothy saw the spider get the furthest it had got so far.

**Maybe that is what I need to do.
I need to find another way.
I need to ask for advice on how to use
that device. I will eventually succeed."**

"That spider isn't giving up Mum. It just keeps trying, even when it slips all the way back again, even when trying seems pointless. It has moved around the bath and tried different approaches.

"Oh Timothy, I am so proud of you!" beamed Timothy's mum.
Timothy started to chant, "You can do it, just keep trying, you are almost there…"

The spider had to take just a few more steps and it would achieve its goal of escaping the bath.

The spider had almost reached the top of the bath and Timothy and his mum held their breath with anticipation.

The last few steps were fast and the spider managed to achieve success.

"Yes! Yes! I knew the spider would succeed eventually; the spider never gave up even when it seemed impossible to succeed. It tried another way and eventually succeeded."

Timothy looked at his mum and said, "I shall be like the spider and I know I will succeed eventually."

Did you know?

Spiders eat pests.

Did you know?

There are approximately 40,000 spiders worldwide.

Did you know?

Spiders have 8 legs.

Did you know?

Old spider webs are called cobwebs.

Did you know?

Spiders are arachnids, not insects.

Did you know?

Insects have six legs.

Did you know?

These are the pictures of the spider in the bathroom.

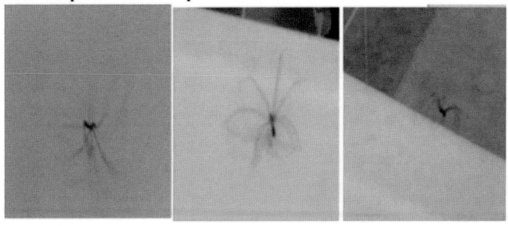

ABOUT THE AUTHOR

Cally Finsbury and Timothy Finsbury are a writing team.

Made in the USA
Monee, IL
23 November 2019